Dear Parents:

Congratulations! Your child is taking the first steps on an exciting journey. The destination? Independent reading!

STEP INTO READING® will help your child get there. The program offers five steps to reading success. Each step includes fun stories and colorful art or photographs. In addition to original fiction and books with favorite characters, there are Step into Reading Non-Fiction Readers, Phonics Readers and Boxed Sets, Sticker Readers, and Comic Readers—a complete literacy program with something to interest every child.

Learning to Read, Step by Step!

Ready to Read **Preschool–Kindergarten**
• big type and easy words • rhyme and rhythm • picture clues
For children who know the alphabet and are eager to begin reading.

Reading with Help **Preschool–Grade 1**
• basic vocabulary • short sentences • simple stories
For children who recognize familiar words and sound out new words with help.

Reading on Your Own **Grades 1–3**
• engaging characters • easy-to-follow plots • popular topics
For children who are ready to read on their own.

Reading Paragraphs **Grades 2–3**
• challenging vocabulary • short paragraphs • exciting stories
For newly independent readers who read simple sentences with confidence.

Ready for Chapters **Grades 2–4**
• chapters • longer paragraphs • full-color art
For children who want to take the plunge into chapter books but still like colorful pictures.

STEP INTO READING® is designed to give every child a successful reading experience. The grade levels are only guides; children will progress through the steps at their own speed, developing confidence in their reading.

Remember, a lifetime love of reading starts with a single step!

To my sons, Keve and Wes
—R.M.

Visit us on the Web!
StepIntoReading.com
randomhousekids.com

Educators and librarians, for a variety of teaching tools, visit us at
RHTeachersLibrarians.com

ISBN 978-1-5247-6384-8 (trade) — ISBN 978-1-5247-6385-5 (lib. bdg.)

Printed in the United States of America

10 9 8 7 6 5 4 3 2 1

STEP INTO READING®

nickelodeon

by Renee Melendez
based on the teleplay "The Polar Derby"
by Morgan von Ancken
illustrated by Dave Aikins

Random House New York

Blaze and AJ
are ready to race
through the snow.

Blaze turns himself
into a race car
for the Polar Derby.

Zeg, Starla,
Stripes, and Darington
are also race cars!

Blaze wants to win
the Ice Trophy.

Crusher wants
to beat Blaze.

On your marks,
get set, *snow*!
The race begins.

Crusher tries
to cheat!
Blaze, watch out
for the snowball!

Blaze pours on
the speed
to catch up!

Crusher has
a new plan.
He wakes up
some polar bears
to slow down Darington!

Blaze races
to rescue Darington.
They block
the polar bears
with a boulder.

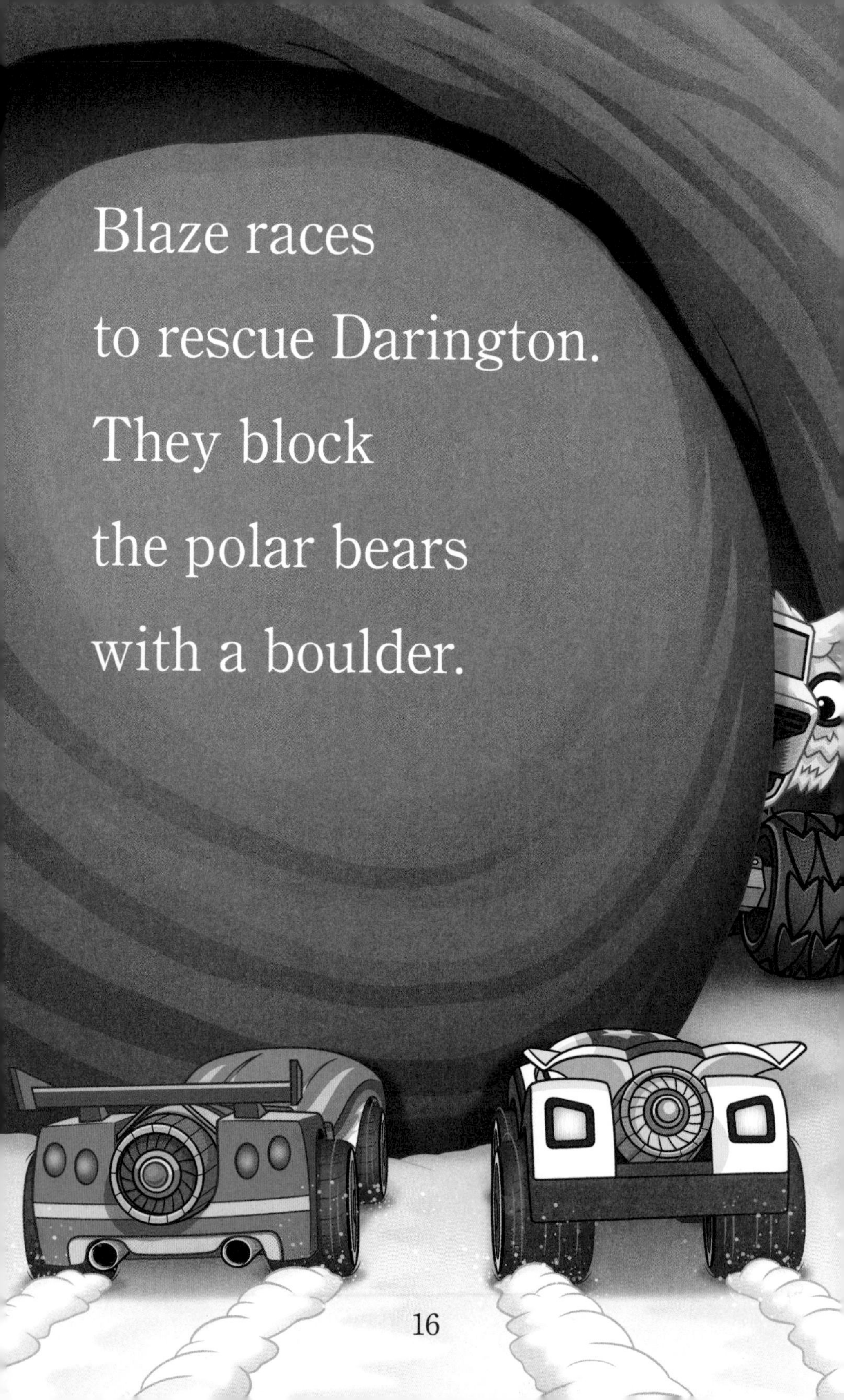

Blaze and Darington
see rocks shaped
like snowboards.
They hop onto an ice track
to slide back
into the race!

Crusher makes
a messy machine.

Balls of snow, cheese, and chocolate roll toward the racers!

Blaze turns himself into a Heat-Cannon Race Car!

He quickly melts
the yucky balls.

Blaze and his friends

use teamwork to get

past the messy machine.

Soon they see

the finish line!

Vroom!

The racers zip past

Crusher.

Blaze and his friends win!

What a *cool* race!